Hello, you!

Oh, please don't **look** inside the pages of this **book**.

Turn around and
quickly **run** ...

The SCHOOL of MONSTERS has begun!

THIS BOOK
BELONGS TO

Mitchell

SCHOOL OF MONSTERS

By Sally Rippin

FRANK IS A BIG HELP

Art by Chris Kennett

Kane Miller
A DIVISION OF EDC PUBLISHING

Some monsters are short, and others are **tall**,

but Frank is quite clearly
the tallest of **all**.

His shoulders are huge, and his arms are quite long.

He's terribly big, and he's terribly **strong**.

But when monsters are making a sculpture for **art**,

DINK
DINK

6

Frank taps at his work,
and it all falls **apart!**

When drawing a picture,
Frank pushes so **hard** ...

... the crayons go flying and land in the **yard**.

The worst is in dancing, with monsters in **pairs.**

SQUISH!

Poor Frank runs away and hides under the **stairs**.

asks the school
gardener, who cares
for their pets.

13

"I'm too tall," says Frank. "I can never fit **in**."

He screws up his face,
and he sticks out his
chin.

"Oh, nonsense!"
she says. "You are
just who I **need**.

Come help me outside. I have babies to **feed**.”

"Babies?" cries Frank.
"No way, I'm too **big**."

"Ha ha!" laughs the gardener. "You must meet our ...

... pig!"

When Frank sees
the babies, he giggles
with **joy**.

The pig has had two:
a girl and a **boy**.

He sits with the piglets tucked into his lap,

and sings them a
song so that Ma Pig
can **nap**.

"Thank you, dear Frank.
I'm run off my **feet**.

You're great with the babies. So gentle and **sweet**.

SNIFFLE

SNUFFLE

"Come when you like,
I'll give you a **job**.

There's not just the babies, but Bill, Barb, and **Bob**."

Frank grins with pride, his heart ready to **burst**.

His day turned out fine
when he'd thought it
the **worst**.

Frank's just right for dancing,

and just right for **art**,

but what matters
the most is the size
of his **heart**!

need

job

in

all

nets

art

burst

stairs

big

yard

long

chin

boy

nap

apart

feed

worst

sweet

Bob

tall

pets

strong

HOW TO USE THIS BOOK

for adults reading with children

Welcome to the School of Monsters!

Here are some tips for helping your child learn to read.

At first, your child will be happy just to listen to you read aloud. Reading to your child is a great way for them to associate books with enjoyment and love, as well as to become familiar with language. Talk to them about what is going on in the pictures and ask them questions about what they see. As you read aloud, follow the words with your finger from left to right.

Once your child has started to receive some basic reading instruction, you might like to point out the words in **bold**. Some of these will already be familiar from school. You can assist your child to decode the ones they don't know by sounding out the letters.

As your child's confidence increases, you might like to pause at each word in bold and let your child try to sound it out for themselves. They can then practice the words again using the list at the back of the book.

After some time, your child may feel ready to tackle the whole story themselves. Maybe they can make up their own monster stories, too!

Sally Rippin is one of Australia's best-selling and most-beloved children's authors. She has written over 50 books for children and young adults, and her mantel holds numerous awards for her writing. Best known for her *Billie B. Brown*, *Hey Jack!* and *Polly and Buster* series, Sally loves to write stories with heart, as well as characters that resonate with children, parents, and teachers alike.

HOW TO DRAW FRANK

① Using a pencil, start with 2 circles for eyes. Add eyebrows, a small nose, and a happy mouth. Draw a big **U** shape for his head.

② Now add a clump of hair and 2 lopsided ears. Then draw 2 curved sides and a belt across his middle.

③ Add 2 rounded shoulders with sleeves, and 2 square shapes for his shorts.

④ Now draw 2 strong arms and 2 big boots.

(5) Draw connecting lines for his legs and the belt loops. Add more lines on his boots, arms, and head, then draw in a belt buckle.

(6) Time for the final details! Draw 2 lines on his sleeves, and add stitches on his arms and head. Add circles to his boots. Don't forget the scar on his cheek!

Chris Kennett has been drawing ever since he could hold a pencil (or so his mom says). But professionally, Chris has been creating quirky characters for just over 20 years. He's best known for drawing weird and wonderful creatures from the *Star Wars* universe, but he also loves drawing cute and cuddly monsters – and he hopes you do too!

WELCOME
TO THE
SCHOOL OF MONSTERS

SCHOOL OF MONSTERS
By Sally Rippin
MARY HAS THE BEST PET
Art by Chris Kennett

You shouldn't bring a pet to school
But Mary's pet is super **cool!**

Have you read ALL the School of Monsters stories?

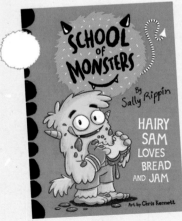

SCHOOL OF MONSTERS
By Sally Rippin
HAIRY SAM LOVES BREAD AND JAM
Art by Chris Kennett

Sam makes a mess
when he eats **Jam.**
Can he fix it?
Yes, he **can!**

SCHOOL OF MONSTERS
By Sally Rippin
PETE'S BIG FEET
Art by Chris Kennett

Today it's Sports Day
in the **sun.**
But do you think that
Pete can **run?**

Jamie Lee sure likes to **eat**! Today she has a special **treat** ...

When Bat-Boy Tim comes out to **play**, why do others run **away**?

Some monsters are short, and others are **tall**, but Frank is quite clearly the tallest of **all**!

When Will gets nervous, he lets out a **stink**. But what will all his classmates **think**?

All that Jess touches gets gooey and **sticky**. How can she solve a problem so **tricky**?

No one likes to be left **out**. This makes Luna scream and **shout**!

Now that you've learned to read along with Sally Rippin's School of Monsters, meet her other friends!

Hey Jack!

Billie B. Brown

Down-to-earth, real-life stories for real-life kids!

Billie B. Brown is brave, brilliant and bold, and she always has a creative way to save the day!

Jack has a big heart and an even bigger imagination. He's Billie's best friend, and he'd love to be your friend, too!

Frank is a Big Help

First American Edition 2022
Kane Miller, A Division of EDC Publishing

Text copyright © 2022 Sally Rippin
Illustration copyright © 2022 Chris Kennett
Series design copyright © 2022 Hardie Grant Children's Publishing
First published in 2022 by Hardie Grant Children's Publishing
Ground Floor, Building 1, 658 Church Street Richmond,
Victoria 3121, Australia.

For information contact:
Kane Miller, A Division of EDC Publishing
5402 S 122nd E Ave, Tulsa, OK 74146
www.kanemiller.com
www.myubam.com

Library of Congress Control Number:
2021949189

ISBN: 978-1-68464-483-4

Printed in China through
Asia Pacific Offset

10 9 8 7 6 5 4 3 2 1